Never Love a Gambler

The New Directions Pearls

Never Love a Gambler

•

KEITH RIDGWAY

A NEW DIRECTIONS PEARL

Manufactured in the United States of America
New Directions Books are printed on acid-free paper.
First published as a Pearl (NDP1295) by New Directions in 2014
Design by Erik Rieselbach
Set in Albertina

Library of Congress Cataloging-in-Publication Data

Ridgway, Keith, 1965–
Never love a gambler / Keith Ridgway.
pages cm
ISBN 978-0-8112-2294-5 (alk. paper)
I. Title.
PR6068.I287N48 2014
823'.914—dc23   2014003583

10 9 8 7 6 5 4 3 2 1

New Directions Books are published for James Laughlin
by New Directions Publishing Corporation
80 Eighth Avenue, New York 10011

Contents

NEVER LOVE A GAMBLER

Never Love a Gambler

THERE WAS THE ROAR of a bus, a shuddering agitation in the warm air, and then a rotten smell that came wafting in the open door from the street, and then a second later a dog, an awful nightmare of a dog, a cur, who strolled by with something dead in the clamp of his jaw.

"Ah Jaysus," moaned Dodo, hiding her eyes. "What's he got? What's he got?"

The dog went on, dripping, and there was a trail left after him, of something dark and thick that was not blood.

"A rat I think," said Jimmy, squinting.

"Or a cat. A little kitten."

Another bus roared away from the lights and Dodo picked up her half of stout and put it down again. Jaysus. The smell lingered. It hung and she could see it, a red-black colour like a winter nosebleed. In her leg the pain began. She glanced at her son and burst into tears.

"Ah Mam, don't cry for Christ's sake. What's wrong with you?"

She put down the glass and pulled a sky-blue handkerchief from her pocket and blew her nose and dabbed at her eyes and picked up the glass again and drank. A skinny drunk woman looked down at her sideways from the counter of the bar.

"Nothing," she said.

"Is it Da?"

His father, his father. Her son and his father and the pain in her leg.

"No."

"What then?"

"My leg hurts."

"Is that it?"

"Feels like there's something living in me knee. It's killin' me Jimmy. Turns and twists and turns like it can't get asleep."

"We'll go to the doctor tomorrow."

"What do you want to go for?"

"You go on your own so."

"He's useless."

"He's all right."

"He looks down at me, turns up his nose."

She drank, and watched him out of the corner of her eye as he stuck a finger in his whiskey and sucked it. Her knee twisted itself again and she scrunched up her face and stuck out her tongue and let a moan out of her till it passed.

"All right Dodo?" the barman called.

"Oh yes. It's me knee. Awful in the heat."

"Awful in the cold. Awful in the in-between," said

Jimmy huffily, his eyes front ahead, his mess of hair in a greasy tumble over the bad skin of his forehead. Forehead from his father. Great domes the two of them—made you think of clever, complicated men. They weren't that.

"I'd have thought it'd be better when it's dry," said the barman. "Dry and hot like it is. I thought the damp'd be worse."

"No," said Dodo, conscious of Jimmy smiling and shaking his head.

The barman lit a cigarette and flicked the flame from his match and tossed it smoking towards the door, but it fell short, landing on the colourless mat.

"Joints are awful things," he said. "Never trust them."

Dodo nodded and stared into her stout. Jimmy watched the barman for a while and then lit a cigarette of his own, drawing in a great big lungful of smoke and pausing for a long moment and hurling it out of him then in a great big rush towards the bright street.

"I wonder is it cigarettes?" said Dodo.

"You've been off them for years."

"Not as long as I was on them. Rose Kelly's sister-in-law had a leg amputated and she was on forty a day and I was on forty a day too."

Jimmy said nothing, only shook his head and drew again the soft grey smoke into himself and held it, as if it were necessary to test something, in his insides.

"There's that dog," said Dodo, and Jimmy breathed out.

"He's eaten it."

"Ah don't say that."

"Swallowed it whole."

"It's a fierce smell off him."

The dog paused in the doorway and looked in, one eye gooey and the other colourless and blind. His coat was dirty with dust and filth and he was of no particular breed. A scar ran down one side, and he dragged that hind leg, and he smelled hugely.

"Poor fella," said Dodo. "Bad leg too."

"Forty a day man."

Dodo smiled.

At the other end a door opened and in stepped Mossie Russell, and all the bar glanced up at him and away again, and there was a slight hush, all eyes. The skinny woman got up and left, going out the side door, stepping, almost falling, over the old dog who now lay panting on the pavement staring at Dodo.

"Shite," muttered Jimmy, cleared his throat, shifted in his seat.

Mossie Russell walked smiling across the room, for all the world like he had stepped out of a game show, as if there was applause going on, as if he was delighted, delighted, to be here, my word, with all these lovely, lovely people. He nodded hugely at the barman and made a gun with his finger and fired it, clicking in his mouth, just a couple of times too often, so that it was funny, or past funny, a parody of that type of man, so that he showed that he had the measure of himself, contained himself, stood beside himself, watched you watching, letting you know he was cleverer than he seemed, but keeping a secret still just how much cleverer, as if the parody might itself be a joke, a double cross, a parody of your smug amusement, a way of getting at you no matter who you were or what you thought. Here was Mossie Russell. And without once glancing at them as far as Dodo could see, he strode the length of the place in his swagger and came straight to her and Jimmy. He clapped his hands and rubbed them.

"Mrs Fitzgerald," he said. "Jimmy," he said. He smiled at them and held his arms out wide and stood like that for a moment, a beaming cruciform shape, an exaggeration of himself, tempting comment. Jacket a kind of yellow. Go on. Say a word.

He sat at their table on a low stool with his back to the door and the dog. "Mind if I join yous?" This after he was seated.

"We do yes," said Jimmy.

"Ah shut up Jimmy," said Mossie, delighted. "What are yous havin'?"

"I'm fine thanks," said Dodo, chewing, which was what she did.

"Jimmy?"

"What?"

"What can I get you?"

"Large Black Bush."

Mossie laughed and nodded at the barman. He reached into the pocket of his jacket then and pulled out a box of

Extra Mild Silk Cut and a gold lighter and offered cigarettes to Dodo, who shook her head, and to Jimmy, even though he had one lit. Jimmy took one and dropped it into his shirt pocket. Mossie laughed again.

"You're great fuckin' fun Jimmy do you know that? What's that fuckin' smell?"

"It's the dog," said Dodo quickly, and nodded her head towards the open door. Mossie turned and looked and stood up then and went over to the dog and aimed a kick. But the dog had seen him coming and got out of the way with a speed that was shocking for a dog in his state. Gone he was.

Mossie came back to the table shrugging his jacket and nodding, as if acclaimed. Squinting eyes brought on by smiling. Smiling brought on by squinty eyes. The barman put down a pint and a large whiskey and went off again without asking for money.

"Grand," said Mossie, sitting on the stool. "Are you sure Mrs Fitzgerald that you won't have another?"

"No thanks Mossie. I'm fine now."

"Right."

He fell silent and stared at the table, and Dodo looked at the horseshoe of hair that sat on the top of his head, and at the taut honey-coloured scalp that he scratched now, as if her gaze was an irritation. He looked up at the ceiling and rubbed his chin and his throat, and Dodo looked at the two rings that he wore on his left hand and then glanced at his right hand that rested on the table top and saw the three rings there, and looked at his neck, expecting to see a chain, but seeing no such, just a tuft of dark hair poking out from under his black denim shirt. He wore a yellow, well, sandy, mustard, she wasn't sure, sports jacket, and black jeans and a big buckled belt and soft brown shoes. There was a scent from him that was fresh and clean, and he held his cigarette between his pale fingers as if it was a permanent fixture, forgotten. But then, her irritant eyes again, he took a drag and blew the smoke upwards, away from her.

"Isn't this the weather?" he asked.

Dodo nodded. Jimmy scowled.

"It's global warming," said Mossie. "Global warming. The sun goes lethal and we get more of it. Get worse before it gets better. And of course some fools lap it up. Always have. Billy Lawlor from Phibsboro out on the grass in his knickers the first sign of it. That's some sight. Every time Mrs Sullivan looks out her window there he is spread-eagled like he's fallen off the roof, his shite brown legs and his scrawny body. She complains about it but you know I think it's the only reason she listens to the weather forecast. Makes sandwiches the night before if it's going to be hot. Sits there all day long drinking diet coke and munching her sambos, her eyes crawling all over Billy Lawlor's sorry corpse."

He gave a great laugh, winked at Dodo, sipped his golden drink.

"Then Mrs Grealy calls by and wants to see the new

wallpaper in the upstairs bedroom, new since 1979, and they sit there the two of them making Billy Lawlor wonder why he's so bleedin' itchy. I'm a winter man. Warm coats and coal fires and hot drinks. But some people. Lie in the fuckin' sun from dawn to dusk and not move a muscle. I never understood it. Jetting off to Spain and fuckin' Florida. When I go away I go to cities. I go for the culture."

He gave a wide smile and nodded. Roar of the fuckin' crowd.

"Paris. Venice. Rome. Travelling to the sun is a fuckin' joke. If you're looking for a holiday Jimmy take your mother to Paris. Take Mrs Fitzgerald to the Louvre."

He took a drag of the cigarette and stared at Jimmy.

"It's an art museum. Mona Lisa."

"I know."

"Mona Lisa, Mrs Fitz. About the size of a postcard. Big throng of nips around her yapping away. Mona Lisa and the way she might look at you. There's better pictures there. Better stuff than that."

He sighed as if it was a great shame. He looked at his watch.

"Can't find Frank," he said.

Dodo's knee twitched and she gasped and closed her eyes.

"What is it Mrs Fitz?" asked Mossie.

"My leg. My knee."

"Hurts does it?"

She looked at him. His face that he lived in. His face

that he pulled around and pushed at, him behind it some-where, a skeleton with a smell, an earthy breath of bad thoughts. He could stay looking at you with the same ex-pression for a long time, unflinching. While inside he ran around the angles. And even when he had not asked a question, he always looked as if he had.

"Yes," she said.

He nodded.

"Where's your husband missus?"

Dodo sighed and sipped from her stout, the thin head gone warm in the heat.

"Why do you want to know?" asked Jimmy, making his voice hard and slow.

"I have business with him."

"What kind of business?"

"He's in the flat," said Dodo.

"What kind of business?"

"I was at the flat. There's no one there."

Dodo shrugged.

"I asked you a question," Jimmy said.

"I'm sorry Jimmy, I missed it. What did you say?"

"What kind of business do you have with my father?"

Mossie looked at the table top and ran his fingers along the edge of it, his cigarette burning low, his rings bright.

"None of your business business." He laughed and looked up. "You know the kind of thing."

He stared at Jimmy, still smiling, and did not blink. Jimmy nodded and looked away. Mossie turned to Dodo.

"I was at the flat. There's no one there."

"Maybe he has the telly on," said Dodo. "Can't hear you. Maybe he's fallen asleep."

Mossie took a last sharp drag from his cigarette and stubbed it out in the ashtray, it hissing in the water and smoking and dying. Mossie drank and put his glass down and folded his arms.

"I thought that," he said. "I thought that might be it. But no. There's no one in the flat at all, asleep or awake."

His smile was gone and Dodo could not look at him.

"What do you mean?" asked Jimmy.

Mossie said nothing.

"Did you break in to our fuckin' flat?"

"Didn't know you still lived with your Mam, Jimmy."

Jimmy made a small hissing noise and Dodo glanced at the ashtray.

"Now Jimmy," said Mossie. "There's no call for that at all. Your Da invited me by not turning up. Me sittin' like a fool on the steps outside the gallery, that's an invitation. Half hour I was there. That's an invitation Jimmy. Given the circumstances."

Jimmy did not say anything. He lifted his whiskey, the one he had bought for himself, and drank it all. The double Black Bush stayed where it was. Mossie watched him and turned again to Dodo.

"Lovely place you have missus. Nice view too, of the world. And you have all the gear. The telly and the video and all that. Deep fat fryer. Microwave."

"We don't have a deep fat fryer," said Dodo.

"Lovely view though. That height."

"I don't know where he is," said Dodo, and she sipped her stout.

Mossie nodded. He traced his fingers on the table top and cleared his throat.

"I've left a fella by the flat in case he comes home. You don't mind him. He's outside the door and he's a nice fella and you won't know he's there. In the meantime if you know where Frank might be, if it occurs to you suddenly like, then I'll be at my place and I'd love to hear from you. Right?"

Dodo nodded.

"Fuck off," said Jimmy.

Mossie stood quickly and his stool fell over behind him and Dodo crouched back out of the way as he leaned across the table and grabbed Jimmy by the shoulder of his shirt and lifted him to his feet, the shirt ripping a little and a button popping out into the air, Dodo watching it, up and across and down like it was taking forever, through the air with her eyes on it all the way, and down then, plop, the sound maybe only in her head, who knows, into the Black Bush like a body in the canal in the sunset. Dodo was stuck on that for a moment. By the time she was back, tugged round by a shaking in the surface like a nice evening breeze, Mossie had pulled Jimmy towards him and the table was pinched by their thighs.

"Now Jimmy. Stop being a thick little shite and keep

your fuckin' mouth shut or we'll have to see how well you dangle. Do you hear me Jimmy?"

His face was so close to Jimmy's, and his voice so loud, as if Jimmy was in another room, that he spat on Jimmy with all the openings and closings of his mouth. Then he was still for a minute, glaring, with not a sound in the place, not even in the street or the whole of the city, so it seemed to Dodo, then he sniffed and let go, and Jimmy dropped to the seat wiping at his mouth.

"Fuck's sake," he muttered.

"I'll be off," said Mossie. He nodded at Dodo and his smile was back. He ran his hand over his head. "I'll see you around Mrs Fitzgerald. See you soon."

He nodded at the barman and walked back through the bar, stopping to talk to a couple at a table by the door, shaking hands with an old fella who stood up for it. He did not look back. Then he was gone, and the barman looked towards Dodo and Jimmy and shook his head slowly.

"Jesus Christ," said Jimmy. "He's a fucking bollox."

"What does that mean?" Dodo asked.

"What?"

"We'll see how well you dangle. What does that mean?"

"They hung a fella off the top of the flats last week. Tied a rope around his ankle and the other end around a chimney stack or something and pushed him off. Fucking left him there. The fire brigade had to come. It's his new thing. Bungee jumping. The fella's leg was nearly ripped out of him."

Dodo drank what was left of her stout. She reached for her stick.

"Come on," she said.

"Where?"

"To find your father."

Jimmy sighed and shook his head, but he did not argue. He fiddled with his shirt, looked for his button, felt the cheap material, patting himself, as if it might have slipped inside and be against his skin. Dodo watched him. As if something would be against his skin. She closed her eyes and told herself that that was a wrong thought. You love your son. Your children. Love.

She was about to tell him where it was, but that would give her away. Let him know that at his moment of danger, his pale body threatened, she, his very mother, had chosen to watch the gentle arc of a plastic button through slow motion air into whiskey. Which was, she thought, shocking. They moved away, her son helping her, a sash of his white stomach visible, the Black Bush staying where it was. She thought of some poor man coming across it and delighting in his good fortune and knocking it back and choking to death on the button of her son's shirt. The barman called "good luck" and Dodo groaned with the pain in her leg and told her son that it would be fine after a minute. Once they got going, she said. Once they got going the pain would fall away.

Outside the evening was still as hot as the day had been and traffic waited at the lights and two children played on the steps of the wax museum. The dog was there, dozing by the wall in a shaft of sunlight. He looked up at them and got to his feet.

"Are you all right Mam?"

"I'm feckin crippled. I'm like that fella."

She stopped and looked at the dog who took a step towards her and wagged its tail.

"We're for the vet's," she said to him. "You and me son. They'll be putting us to sleep soon the two of us."

The dog nodded and turned in a circle and wagged its tail and seemed happy at last. Happy at last. The end of the day and happy at last.

"Where'll we look?" asked Jimmy.

Dodo leaned on her stick and patted the handbag that was slung around her shoulders and pulled her handkerchief from the pocket of her cardigan and dabbed her mouth and her nose.

"I don't know love. We'll go around by the gallery I suppose. By the Garden. Maybe he's over in Barry's."

She set off slowly, taking small steps. The dog watched her, Jimmy held her elbow. She remembered being other than this. Always that memory at the start. Fell away when she got going. Everything falls away when you get going.

After a few yards they moved a little faster. The pain in her leg made itself smaller. The dog followed. At the pedestrian crossing past The Granby, at the corner of the square, the lights were against them. If she stopped she'd have to start again. There was a bus approaching. Always a bus. She shook Jimmy loose and strode across the road against the red man.

"Jaysus Mam. Will ye fuckin' wait."

The bus blew a loud horn and Dodo hurried. The dog ran ahead of her, telescoping its arse up to its ears. Dodo tried something similar, regretted it, something in her hips clicking.

"If I stop it'll hurt," she said.

"If you don't stop it'll fuckin' kill you."

The bus had slowed and moved around them. The driver leaned out of his window and shouted.

"Yeah yeah," said Jimmy. "Yeah yeah."

They walked with the dog in tow and the leg pain diminishing, like a toddler rocked silent by travel, leaving off its scratching and its squeaking and fading into sleep. Dodo thought herself a ship with a child aboard, as she had in pregnancy, sailing through all those days of her life like a liner, and the thought made her thirsty again. They went on. Past the school and the parking meters and the cars parked head on, and into the clear space in front of the Hugh Lane Gallery of Modern Art. She squinted at the steps and slowed. Jimmy regarded her with suspicion as she tugged at him and dwindled and came to a stop. They looked at the closed doors.

"He's not here all right," said Jimmy.

"Why meet here?"

She felt her son shrug and mutter something about Mossie and culture. She had met Mossie's mother once, a delicate woman, thin and smoky, a tireless talker, long hands that tapped ash and fear, fear and ash. Dodo stared upwards at the gallery, at first floor windows and then at second floor windows. A face looked down at her. A pale circle in the dusty air. Straight into her eyes. She gripped Jimmy's arm tightly and gasped, and he must have thought that it was her leg at her again because instead of looking up he looked down, at her knee, crouched and stared at it, as if he might catch a spasm, a ripple in the skin, a flutter of the kneecap. Dodo tugged at him, her eyes impatiently wandering for the slightest of seconds, but enough. Enough to lose it. Jimmy straightened and looked where she looked and saw nothing for there was nothing there.

"Oh," said Dodo.

"What is it?"

"Nothing." The dog wet a parking meter and nodded at her. It was his bad leg he lifted. "Let's go on."

They walked, the leg pain oddly quiet. Dodo could not glance back without stopping and they did not stop. The face had been a man's, and Dodo had been sure that he had looked directly at her, and that he was pale and saddened, and that he was dead and a ghost, or a spirit, or a memory in her own mind of a previous life, shone up on the glass of the window like a cinema or an old party trick from her days as a girl. Or perhaps God, or the devil, or a murdered soul, trapped, or an angel. One of those many things.

"What was that house?"

"What house?"

"The gallery. Who lived there before it was a gallery?"

"I don't know Mam. Some old English Lord or something. Maybe. I don't know."

Dodo shuffled, her sore feet scuffing the ground.

"There'd be a lot of history there then."

"Yes."

"All old stories of murders and sad ladies and candles."

Jimmy sighed. He was looking over towards the Garden Of Remembrance.

"There'd be ghosts there too," said Dodo. "Or the hope of ghosts."

She thought of the dead. They would be flighty. They would be cautious like children, like parents, conscious of the difference. They'd know the trouble of living and have soft sighing pity on her. On her and her husband and her sons and her daughters and their children who ran in small circles around her and dizzied her with giggling. They'd watch, the dead. She raised her eyes and sniffed the air. Over by the cross pool and the children of Lir. Ghosts. The uncertainty of them. Marks on the ground for them. Signs they might know. Calling out to them. Come here and hover. We shaped you a pool.

"Barry's Ma?"

"We might as well have a look."

They passed the tall mast of Findlater's church and waited at the lights this time, her leg very calm. Jimmy monitored her. The dog sat politely, its raggy coat splayed on the ground, some connection made in its simple brain between Dodo and the scent of its dreams. They crossed and she thought of sending Jimmy into the shop for a can of something, but said nothing and they went on into Gardiner Row and the high lights. It was gloomy now, the sun sickening behind them. They walked to the crack in the pavement that marked the end of Gardiner Row and the start of Great Denmark Street. She waited on the footpath with the dog, a hand on the black railings, while Jimmy ran into Barry's. She watched a grey-dressed schoolboy slowly idle by her, his big eyes on the ground. They were back then. Poor things.

"Back already?" she said.

He heard her. She knew he'd heard her. It was in those big eyes, and in the tiny stiffness of his little head. But he didn't look up. He set his small mouth shut and went by, his hands in his pockets, his schoolbag shrugged up on his narrow back. He was a low thing, not up to her elbow. About eight maybe. First class. New to the middle of the city. Don't talk to strangers.

Dodo let go of the railing and glanced at her palm. Black paint flecked. She gripped things tightly now.

"Were you not collected?" she called to him.

He sort of paused, then continued, as if he'd stepped over a little bump in the ground.

"Belvo is it?

He glanced back. Whatever she was to look at she was

"Very strong love."

He bent his body and picked up his bag and straightened again and was up the door step and down again, three steps ahead, turned, back again, a little jump, reaching his hands up on the wall to feel the wallpaper. Dodo was dizzy. Her knee was building up to a rage. A pure rage.

Behind her there was a little whimper, barely heard. She turned and waved.

"You stay there boy. We'll be back in a minute." Mossie the dog nodded and flopped on the footpath, his chin at rest on two soft paws. Dodo envied that. Wished she could settle down for a snooze.

"There's the phone Ma."

She stuck out her hand and Jimmy rummaged in his pocket and blew out a breath and Dodo didn't breathe in while it flowed by her. The boy was looking happier now. He swayed on his little legs. A couple came by them, arm in arm, going in. A barman swung a bunch of keys and nodded at Jimmy and glanced at the boy and went through glass doors whistling.

"What's the number love?"

He told her, one number at a time, as she pressed the buttons and heard the tones in her ear. It rang. And rang. No one exactly sitting by the phone. Then it opened onto air, a hiss, a space. A sleepy man's voice said, "Hello there." Her knee was on the verge of bursting.

"Hello. Mr …" She held her hand over the mouthpiece. "What's your surname love?"

"Hickey."

"Mr Hickey. My name is Dodo Fitzgerald …"

"Who?"

"Dodo Fitzgerald. I'm here with …"

"Dodo?"

"Yes. I'm here with your son. With Killin. Oh sweet Jesus Christ!"

It was her knee. It buckled and flexed like a fish. Something electric shot up her thigh and spewed a thick syrupy pain through her bowels and her pelvis and her shivering flesh. She vomited pain sounds.

"Hello?"

"Mam? Leg? Here."

Jimmy took the phone while Dodo grabbed her knee and pressed, and backed her backside into the wall. She stood one foot on the other in an effort to confuse her senses. She thought she might faint. Through a dripping mist she saw the boy stare at her with an open mouth, fascinated. Wondering if she'd die maybe. Perhaps thinking of his mother. Dodo bit her cheek. Cried.

"We have your son Mr Hickey. What? No he's not, don't be stupid. You never collected him."

It found a way across her hips, turning them to dust, and shot down the other leg. To the other knee. She was now dying in stereo. Being shot would not be as bad.

"Well whatever. We're at Barry's Hotel on Denmark Street and if you're not here in fifteen minutes we pull the trigger."

And Jimmy hung up. The boy looked at him and Jimmy grinned.

"All right Ma?"

"Don't mind him love he was only joking with your father. Good lord." It echoed through her like a bomb. Everything shook. Her body was a trembling bag of soft fraying strings and bubbles that burst.

"Are you all right?"

"I have a bad knee. It hurts sometimes very badly."

She thought from his half open mouth and his big eyes, blue as it happens, that he was about to say something, perhaps that his mother had had the same complaint and he hoped that Dodo would not die too, and she thought as well that maybe she had the same name as his mother, which was, which was …

"Is my father coming?"

"He is," said Jimmy, looking out the door, lighting a cigarette. "He's coming to get you. Be here soon. Thought someone else was doing it. Fuckin' mortified."

Jimmy showing off in front of a child, swaggering, being like a film star with his cigarette, spitting towards the dog. Dodo leaned on the wallpaper, swung her leg from the knee, eased it like turning on a cold tap. She limped to the door and across to the steps, past Jimmy and his smells. The boy followed, scurried to the footpath like a dancer, offered her a white hand. Gentleman.

"Good fella. Thank you love. I need to pace. It calms the soreness."

"Did you fall?"

The dog was on its feet, watching her carefully. Ready to catch her. It was easier going down. No sign of Jimmy.

She put her weight on the little man. He took it.

"No. Thank you love. That's it. There we are. It grew on me. Crept up."

"Like a ghost."

"Exactly like that."

"Where did you see a ghost?"

"I'm not sure love. In an old house maybe. It was probably just a cleaner. A man looking out the window. It was probably just that."

He nodded. She thought that he would have pondered death. That ghosts would have a hold on him in more than just the scary way. That he might have seen his mother in the dark of his bedroom just before the dawn.

"Have you ever seen a ghost?"

"No."

He had forgotten crying. He lugged his bag and paced with her, turning at the end of the railings and coming back, turning again opposite Jimmy, the dog keeping up for a while then sitting at the kerb, puzzled at this nonsense.

They talked. He held back a bit when it came to his new school. He seemed undecided. He seemed to think it very old, odd, as if he had stepped into the past. "The classes have funny names. Some of the teachers wear gowns." She nodded, uncertain. Had no advice for that kind of thing. She told him about her children and their schools. Smoking rooms and clatter palaces. Stained, drizzling places to which she was occasionally summoned to be sneered at in words only understood later. "Your daughter's behaviour is inappropriate Mrs Fitzgerald." Much later. Told him Jimmy had cried his eyes out for days when he first went to school, which was not quite true, though nearly, there having been at that time in her family's life a general wailing, unconnected to circumstances, as far as she could remember, beyond the front door. The child chewed on the news, glanced back at Jimmy with a little admiration and a little understanding. He told her that he had two sisters and a brother who was nearly a doctor. That was nice. Told her that they lived in Clontarf, and he could see the sea from his room. She sighed at that, thought it lovely. Told her that he was a good swimmer, probably the best in all of Elements. And probably better than anyone in Rudiments as well. As good as that? Yes. Told her that his father was a businessman. And that he was left-handed (this information was half whispered), and that he took the boy and his two sisters to the cinema practically every week. Popcorn sickness was a family ailment. Told her that his friend in Clontarf, Paul, had fallen off a wall and broken a cheekbone. He had touched it and felt a soft mushy give, and he shuddered slightly as he recalled it. Said Paul had screamed his head off.

About his mother, nothing.

"My mother," said Dodo, trying to remember, "was a singer."

Silence. The dog was yawning.

"She sang old songs that you wouldn't know. Was an angel at a party or a wedding or a funeral or any class of gathering at all. She met my father in a chorus line. He was a chorus boy. She was a chorus girl. They fell in love and lived in Primrose Street. Music always. I had four brothers and two sisters. We were always fed and clothed and cared for. She lived to nearly ninety. She did. My mother."

Nothing. Then he sighed. Rubbed at his nose.

"My mother left us."

"She what?" It was a way of saying it surely?

"She left. She had this problem and she had to go away for it. Not to jail or anything, but she couldn't stay because it wasn't good for her to stay. Or for us. Or something."

Well. She stood still for a moment, paused. Felt a tension start in her knee, a turning of a clammy screw. Looked at the light on the head of the boy. Moved off again.

"That's very sad."

He gave his sigh.

"She writes."

What did she write?

"Liked a drink did she?"

"No, not really."

Well. Dodo frowned and tried to work it out. A lover. But her children? Was the woman maybe dead and the left-handed father and the doctor son telling lies and forging letters? Maybe she really was in jail. Though probably a lover. So easily found these days. So easily taken. A lover. A bright flame in a far town. Perhaps there was, oh, she knew, a breakdown. A mental collapse. An asylum.

"How long ago did she leave?"

"I don't know. A few years."

Could a mad woman write letters?

They turned and came towards Jimmy again. Mulling things over. The boy seemed to whisper, or hum. Dodo tried to hear, but it was hard, above the traffic from the square, and the odd car that passed them, and the one or two people, and the planes in the sky. Jimmy cursed. Dodo looked at him frowning, fed up with his bare belly and his nicotine and his sharp skull. But he was staring off down the street nervously. Dodo looked. The night almost down. Figures in the gloom, moving into the light's glow, one of them briefly open-armed, as if advancing on an embrace. Not a specific embrace. A general embrace. The glad arms of many. Mossie Russell.

He sauntered. Up the street from Findlater's church as if the path disappeared behind him, a cigarette in his hand, a big thug at each shoulder, two thieves. Brutish shadows and Mossie bringing light. In the sky there was a red line like a cut on a black man. The evening smell. The chill air. Mossie dropped his arms and changed his tune. Slightly hunched now, not a television colour any longer but a late night black and white gangster, bright grey but for the red gash in the skin of the sky.

"You wait here love," Dodo told the child, pressing him back a little so that he leaned against the railings. She moved away. Moved forward. Halted. Mossie in the open air at night time was not a thing she'd choose. Jimmy was small in the door, not crouching, but small. Mossie Russell said something to his entourage. There was a nod.

"Mrs Fitz." He stopped and beamed at her.

"No luck then?" Dodo asked in a shakeless voice.

"No." He seemed delighted. "Nor you?"

"No."

"Isn't that an awful shame?"

He was beside her, laid an arm across her shoulders, turned her gently to face the road, her back to her son. His party was lost to her, just shapes pushing gently at the air on her back.

"Not sight nor sign. Odd how a man like your Frank can be so, so, ubiquitous, that's the word, then gone. Gone! Like a ghost! Flitted away into the cracks in the ground. Like a ghost! Whoooosh! Poor Mrs Fitz."

Behind them there was the sound of a scuffle, Jimmy cursing, protesting, flapping. Mossie's voice dropped into confidence. Between you and me.

"I'm just taking Jimmy off to the flat Mrs Fitz. You don't come home for a while now all right?"

She nodded God forgive her. Nodded in the smoky light. From the corner of her eye she could see the boy, still as a pillar, small as a bead.

"We'll just see about settling Frank's account via a fair estimation of goods and such like. Nothing excessive I assure you. Sort out the whys and wherefores at a later date. No need to worry yourself. Suffices tonight to reach a round figure in terms of items in lieu. Need Jimmy for, eh, for guidance."

Jimmy squealed like a pig in a dream and Dodo turned just enough to see his arm twisted up behind his back and his face in a scrunch. The gap in his shirt had grown bigger. It seemed to hold a patch of the ground. He was marched by one of the big men back down towards Parnell Square. His insect shadow attached to a tree.

"Don't do that thing with him," said Dodo.

"What thing?"

"Dangling or whatever."

Mossie looked at her. Looked into her eyes. Sucked his cigarette.

"OK."

She nodded, but it was the way he held her gaze. It was too straight. Too solid. Honest and sincere and his word as a gentleman. Liar.

The dog brushed her leg. The second big man was out of sight. Somewhere back there, hands held loosely at his crotch, chewing probably, looking this way and that. Under control Mr Russell. Again the brush of the dog and a waft of his decay. Mossie made a face. Looked down. Made a blubbery noise, shooed at the creature. The creature persisted.

Dodo glanced. And then, oh then, in the night that had finally fallen, with the cold air lapping her shoulders, Dodo heard, and it stopped all the clocks in her faltering world, the thin lovely voice of the boy.

"Mossie. Mossie. Come here."

She opened her mouth to gasp or gape, or something. But her mouth caught the city and tasted the slowness of all things, the patience of time.

"Come here Mossie. Come here."

Mossie the man let her go. Stood and peered into the gloom by the railings. Mossie the dog stayed where he was, looked up at Dodo. Dodo wondered at the sloth of sudden things. How they unravel.

Mossie the man stepped towards the boy, who cowered.

"What?" said Mossie. Astonishment really. The heavy squinting too. The boy shifted slightly. Straightened. Took stock of the state of things, his place in the world, decided now might be a good time to be more than he felt he was.

"I was not talking," said the brave, brave boy, "to you. I was talking," and here he flung out his small exasperated arm, "to the dog."

Dodo saw it all as if she was a ghost, hovering in living space, watching the play of small mistakes, the breath of lives, the teasing out of moments.

"Fuckin' cheek," said Mossie and grabbed the little stick of flesh and pinned it to the black iron, and raised an arm of his own, and swept his hand down twice, the first time only brushing the boy's hair, the second time harder, the second time coinciding, (and here is where Dodo came into her useless own, seeing all things from all angles without moving an inch), coinciding with the appalling arrival of sharp brakes, the Jimmy squeal of them, the opening of a car door, the flashing run of a strange man, eyes lit in fury, his raised left arm crashing past Dodo towards Mossie the man, just as a shout rings out—"BOSS!" or something—and Mossie turns and seems to arch in the air and come down somewhere else, his shoulder sinking into the man's ribs, the man faltering, the brute shadow arriving with a downward crash of doubled fists and a quick upwards kick to the man's lowered head, the man collapsing, Mossie cursing, Mossie kicking, the brutal shadow kicking, both of them kicking, the dog a mess of barking, the boy a huddle on the cold ground (Dodo watching, altered into infinity, as if the scene is a show in the heavens, the hells), the wretched flexing of the man on the hard ground, his head cracking, his back strangely shaped, Mossie kicking after his shadow has stopped, the shadow taking Mossie's arm, telling him to leave it, "LEAVE IT!" Mossie patting down his hair, leaving it, cursing, kicking again one last time, the boy jerking, the father jerking, Mossie and his shadow leaving, leaving, walking off, Mossie spitting, tugging at his sleeves, tugging at his sleeves, a groaning from the body on the ground, the pool, the boy moving closer, his hands unnaturally stiff, pale, his white face holding nothing, and then from somewhere else, a gentle crash, seen without turning, a meshing of metal and a sprinkling of glass as the father's abandoned car rolls, with all the time in the world, as if everything, absolutely everything, is inevitable, written down and predetermined, into a parked white van with a side of gothic black lettering which reads "Charlemont Catering. Fine Food For Formal And Informal Functions. Business Lunches A Speciality."

Mossie and his men were gone. The dog ceased barking

and sniffed at the beaten man until Dodo chased it away. It. The boy sobbed and held his father's hand. There was a red mark on his shocked alabaster skin, where Mossie's hand had found him. He sat on the ground with his feet before him. A small crowd gathered. Someone called for an ambulance. By the time it had arrived Dodo was on the ground too, her knee a roaring furnace, her eyes scorched, her hand on the poor child's head, her voice ragged in the night, her mind a haul of wrong turns and missed chances and good ideas she had forgotten.

"Blast you Frank Fitzgerald," she cried. "I hope he finds you and I hope he hangs you and I hope it snaps, the rope, I hope it does, I pray to God the rope will snap."

And in the gentle night, the swollen clouds roll across the city. And unlucky dogs bark at empty windows. All falls away when you get going. When you get going it all falls away.

Shame

THIS IS THE START of the story, I know. It is the clearness in my head that tells me. My eyes open slick as fish eyes and I see the world sharp and sudden and my mind is strong this morning. I can feel it. It's cold, but a good cold, on the skin only, no deeper, and I dress fast and steady.

The city is squat. There's a section of it pressed to my window, starting with the river and rising then, up the hill towards the Castle. There's a wetness in the morning, and the sun not working right, hidden in a low place somewhere, not touching us. On the hill by St Audon's there was a fire in the night, an orange glow with crackling that woke the child, who woke us, and we stood by the river and stared up at it for a while until the rain came. Now the fire has left a dirty smudge in the middle of the rooftops, a damp patch, with grey timber pointing out of it, shards and black splinters, and a thin smoke still rising, all the colour gone, as if the night has drained from the day.

By the Custom House I can see two ships that have arrived since last night. They are regular, Liverpool boats, and there are barrel boys running to and from them now, and a bulging crate swinging on the crane a little too wildly, and there are shouts that come to me over the water. The big three-master is gone, though I had seen its shadows and the glow of its watch while we stood staring at the fire only hours since. There is another ship cutting towards the sea now, just passing the lotts.

There is a boat tied to the near bank that I've not seen before. It has a small cabin perched on it like an upturned box and it has a load of wood spilled along its length. There's an ugly man on the deck, drinking from a bottle, talking to my wife who stands with her foot on the hawser, the child at her side, him turned from the river and waving at me. He is five now and curly headed and clever as I am. He does not smile as he waves, but squints an eye at me like he knows something I don't and he's seeing me in a new light. I nod and move from the window and try to find some food.

I have dreamed of eavesdropping now for three nights. I have dreamed of overhearing the noise of the world spun out as a kind of song by a ghost. She was a ghost because I knew her face and the face I knew belonged to my mother. But she was not my mother. She was a ghost with my mother's face. She sang or moaned, I am not sure. She gave off the sound like a scent, a noisome, clicking, pungent wail, and it flowed around me as I hid by a tree in a sunlit field where a silent river winked at me. I choked, and fled, and woke then.

And the next night I listened to my wife, her voice clear and strong and unembarrassed, her words so strange to me that it was a long time before I understood them, understood their meaning, their tight plot. She was discussing my murder with an Englishman. Planning it, working it out. I heard the details that would ensure the rapid decay of my remains, the chemical requirements, what kind of blade, what kind of barrel, a place to place me, a quiet cellar, for three days. Then I would be soup, and they would feed me to the river. The Englishman chuckled, but my wife was businesslike and still, and I awoke as she turned her face and peered into the gloom towards me, and lifted the candle and hissed like a god.

Last night I dreamed of my son. He spoke in his own voice but his words were older, older than I, and though I tried could not make out their meaning. It was English, of that I sure, for there were "ifs" and "ands" and "buts" and once he said "mother" and once he said "father" and once he said "fleece." He sat on the quay, his legs dangling, and he spat once, and I awoke then, in fright, for as his spit arced toward me I knew where I was, that I was in the water.

She's left a pot of tea still hot for me, and dark strong by now as I like it. There's a loaf cut, and a slice of bacon, and I eat a little and drink the tea, hum, and check the pocket watch she keeps in the drawer. It's after eight already and I curse and pull on my boots with my mouth full of bread, and I take my coat and sling it over my shoulder and fill the mug with tea once more and take it out into the day, out to where my wife and son stand by the river.

"Are you late?"

"I am."

"This man has wood to sell."

He looks up at me and his head rises and falls slightly with the water.

"We're not buying wood. We have wood."

I drain my mug and hand it to my wife, and turn and leave a silence behind me, and I can feel their two pairs of eyes on my back, and my son makes three. She has a liking for ugly men, and foreign men of any kind. She takes them to her bed while I am gone and she leaves the boy to wander the house and hear whatever he might, and see whatever he can. I know this to be true because of the strength with which I know it, and because of the evidence.

I walk along the river, quickly. It is not good to be late, even if there will be little enough to do when I get there. I am hailed by men who know me, and I nod at them and gesture, and call out a greeting sometimes, and it is by that means, as if being handed on from voice to voice, from face to face, that I make my way down to the house where the Englishman is kept. It is for him that I work, although I am paid by his employer, and it is to both of them that I appear to be answerable, which is not to my liking, for their relationship has of late been strained. The Englishman is frustrated at the delays, and he is anxious to begin, and he has had enough of plans and drawings and consultations and wishes to get the thing started. So he tries me for information, of which I have none, and is short with me when I can give him no answer. And on the other side, his employer, and mine, blames me for the strain, saying that I am not properly occupying the Englishman, which I feel is a nonsense—I am not employed as a playmate or companion or lady-in-waiting. My job is narrow and I like it that way, and I think that I will throw it all in if it continues in this manner for much longer.

I arrive near the quarter hour, to find that my alternate has left already. I am admitted by a manservant, who smiles at me and is affable and attempts to start a conversation about the night's fire. But I cannot linger, and I knock the door of the gentleman's study and am summoned in, a light sweat on my brow, brought on by my hurrying.

"Good morning Sir."

He grunts and stays where he is, at his desk, writing. He is not genuine in his humours, putting them on and taking them off again like a coat, with a shrug of his shoulders and a flap of his arms. So this morning he is wearing his black mood, and he does not raise his eyes and he writes with a bad tempered hand, and takes up muttering while I stand in front of him and stare at the top of his head. The room is cluttered with books and papers and plans, and instruments of measurement and calculation, and much more besides which I do understand. I believe that he is unproven in his field, which I do not think bodes well for the project, about which I know little but that it involves building a new Custom House and a new bridge and that it is causing upset to a lot of people.

"Are you well Sir?"

"No."

He is a small-framed man, narrow hands, thin hair, eyes are pulsing blue and he takes no notice of his appearance, sitting now this morning in a dirty high-collared shirt and wrapped in a blue robe as if straight from his bed. I cannot see his feet.

"You'll take this letter to Mr Beresford directly."

I raise my eyebrows a little but he's not looking at me at all, he's busy folding and sealing and stamping, and my silence is not worth much to him.

"And you will wait for an answer."

"I'll have the boy go Sir."

He looks at me now.

"You'll go yourself."

I frown at him, at his angry face. My frown is well shaped and says to him that there is nothing to be gained from snarling at me—I am not the cause of his irritation. Directly he sees it he changes his coat of black humour for a hair shirt, for a cloud-grey heavy garment full of weariness and supplication.

"Forgive me, I do not mean to snap at you. But you can understand my frustrations, you can understand my position. It is difficult and tiresome and it does not have a pleasant effect. The letter will read more urgent if it is delivered by you."

"My job is to stay with you Sir, until the evening."

"I will not be alone."

"Nevertheless Sir …"

He sighs and lets his head fall back a little. The room is lit from a window onto the garden, and I can see green leaves leaning on the glass, and I think again about the life I lead, and how it is contained within rooms, and takes place through words and directions, and I wonder whether it is a life at all, and whether it might not be just a dreamed thing, and that I might myself, in my essentials, be elsewhere. For what belongs here?

"I feel like a prisoner," says the gentleman, and I want to smile but do not.

"Indeed Sir."

"So you will not take the letter?"

"I will see to it that it is delivered, and that a reply is awaited, and I will ensure that the urgency is impressed upon Mr Beresford."

He sighs again, and ducks his head now, and scratches it, and yawns.

"All right, all right. See to it."

I take the letter from his hand, and he looks me miserably in the eye, and says nothing, and has nothing to say, and I want to test my notion and I glance at the window and the leaves on the glass and I look back at him and I start to say it but I am stopped by the part of myself which does not allow me to test anything.

"What's that?"

"Time Sir …"

"What of it?"

I am for a moment at a loss.

"Passes quickly," I say, lowly, and I feel my cheeks run red, and feel the damp line still on my forehead, and I wish to be asleep so that I can wake.

He nods, or rather, he lowers his head and raises it again, like that.

"Indeed. Not it seems, Mr Beresford's time."

"Yes Sir."

He regards me as peculiar, as well he might, and I turn and leave him and I see to it that the letter is sent, and that a reply is received, and I walk in the garden and I count the leaves.

I have given the impression that my wife is not trustworthy, and this is not true. She does not take men to her bed when I am gone. She does not allow the child to wander freely while she does it. And yet, there is evidence.

I understand the nature of things by the evidence that is presented to me concerning their substance and their place. Evidence is that which I see and hear which allows me to determine a thing is as it seems to be. I learned this subject from a man I knew in the Americas who had both curiosity and learning, and who, I think, died, in front of my eyes, as a result of a scuffle with an Indian knifeman in the country of Virginia. But he would have cautioned me to be unsure, as I do not have the evidence that he is for certain dead. He was wounded in the chest, and if he lived it would surprise me, knowing what I know of wounds like those, but what do I know about living and dying? Not enough. Never enough. Circumstances did not allow me to linger and to find out.

But of my wife, there is too much evidence. For I dream of her often, and I think of her more, and these dreams and these thoughts show me more than I know by other means, and I cannot, in truth, separate them out and judge one as weightier than the other. So that there is always doubt, and this doubt infects my life with her, and I know that there is no reason to it, but that does not disperse it.

I am no fool. I have seen men torn apart by jealousy, and rage at imagined slights. I am aware of those dangers. These are not things I take on. It is not jealousy that fills me. It is dreams that fill me. Thoughts. Evidence. I see her in the past and in the future, sometimes with me and sometimes not, sometimes alone and benign and faultless, sometimes rank and foul and eager for others. And I know that she does not dream these dreams. I know that she does not plot my death with Englishmen and barrels. I know that she has no plans other than the plans she should have, and that she has no desire to hurt me or to wrong me or to see me dead. But these things exist. I have seen them.

Where do they come from?

It is past midday and the reply from Mr Beresford has cheered my gentleman considerably. I have instructions to escort him in the evening to the site, and to allow him to survey and take measurements and so forth, though I must take my alternate with me, as well as three of Mr Beresford's own men, in convoy, for protection. This is good news for me. It will break the monotony of these days.

There is a caller at the house, a woman who will not give her name. She stands in the reception room and surveys the furniture and the paintings and is haughty and will have no truck with me, though she is not moneyed or grand or impressive. It is the gentlemen she wants to see.

I knock on his door and interrupt him at his soup, which he slurps as I tell him that there is a caller, a lady, who will not tell me her name, but who says she is expected. He is properly dressed now. I can see that already he has grouped together those items he needs for our expedition.

"No. I have no appointments. What does she look like?"

"She is a delicate lady Sir, dark haired, pale skinned."

"Is she pretty?"

I hesitate. I do not find her handsome, but I wonder if he will.

"Well?"

"She is pleasant Sir."

"That's no answer."

I am silent. It is not my job to answer questions like that.

"Oh show her in then."

I am not entirely easy with this. My instructions are to admit civilised callers and to report their visits, but there have been few, and none before who have not either been expected or known to me. When I summon her she gives me a small shake of her head which is intended to scold me for my foolishness. I lead her to his study, and follow her into the room, remaining at the door, behind the precise, cutout shape of her back. He stands, his soup things pushed to one side, and waits for her to speak. She glances behind herself, at me.

"Good day ma'am. How may I help you?"

"You are Mr Gandon?"

"Indeed," he says, shrugging a little.

"I am Mrs Millington."

His face changes. It opens wider, in surprise or shock, I do not know. For a moment he stares at her. And then becomes solicitous, sympathy floods his features, as if the name has evidence hanging from it like ivy. He moves behind his desk, walks towards her, all the time saying, "Mrs Millington, my dear lady, I had no idea you were in Dublin, but of course, how do you do, how do you do, it is an honour ..."

And he shoos me away with a flick of his wrist and an irritated look. I hesitate, but if he is content with her then it is none of my business who she is. I leave them, and the last sight I have of them both is like a painting, I view it like I would a painting, so clear is it, so fixed and certain. He stands slightly to her side, with her hands held in his, and his head is at an angle, inclined towards the window, and he smiles, but a sorrowful smile, as if he wishes to commiserate with her, to condole and to comfort. She stands with her head bowed, staring somewhere towards his chest, accepting his wishes, surrendering herself to his sympathy, giving up her shallow indifference for a shallow kind of grace. I do not like her.

Why do I say that it is the last sight I have of them? For I do not mean that it is the last sight I have of them for the moment, but for ever. This is how it presents itself to me. And yet this is unlikely to be the case, unless I die now and am removed from seeing this daily unfolding of my standard life, my routine life, my measured time.

I go to the kitchens and eat some bread and some cheese, and find a jug of claret and help myself to a glass. A maid flirts with me and I am silent in the face of it and she withdraws, a little sullen, her fingertips gone green from polishing. The kitchen is warm, and it has the look of an older place that has not changed in many years, and it puts me in mind of my boyhood, when I was quiet and still and scolded for it. We had dogs who nuzzled me and snapped at strangers, and they would take me sometimes, to strange parts of the city, to streets and lanes which were at odds with the rest of it, and I would want to return home but the dogs were always onward bound, seeking out cracks in the ground, holes in the walls, tears in the blanket of my little mind. I would think us lost, and be ready to bawl and ask a stranger to take care of me, when the dogs would turn a corner and we would be home, suddenly, as if we had never left it. With my mother or my father I knew where I lived. With the dogs I was never sure.

She has left without my knowing, after spending maybe

an hour with him, or not much more. He is packing two bags now, with instruments and papers and notebooks, and he worries that I have not left enough time to make all the arrangements necessary, and will not listen when I tell him that all is in hand, that my alternate is on his way, that Mr Beresford's men are due at five, that he is not to concern himself with that side of things. Concern himself he does however, and from upstairs somewhere he produces a short sword in a black scabbard, and he confronts my amusement with hoods on his eyes and a grim look and words about chance and importance. It seems to me at first that he inflates the latter, but I am not sure after all, where all of this is leading.

He is impatient to be gone, but there is nothing else to be done—other than to wait for the hour to approach us. He sits with his bags at his feet, his sword hung from his waist, and glances at the sky in the window, and at his pocket watch. It will not rain. I wonder how he would use the sword, and try to draw him out about it, but he is not keen on conversation, preferring to hum and fret and make occasional notes in a moleskin book he keeps in his pocket, licking his pencil more than he needs to and leaving a black line on his lip.

I find him so ridiculous that he scares me somewhat. What is he doing here? I mean in this life, my life. In my city. What are his plans? He has about him an arrogance and surety of purpose which does not seem to fit here. He is come amongst us to alter things, and I cannot frame the alteration properly in my mind, cannot see its reach or its import. Maybe it is nothing.

It is close to five, and my alternate has arrived—I can hear him complaining to the staff about his rest being disturbed. He is a surly man, hard, well suited to looking after our charge during the night, but without much usefulness otherwise.

Our gentleman now wants to be on his way, and I have to persuade him repeatedly that we cannot meet Beresford's men en route, that there is too much chance in it, that we should follow our directions. But they are late, and he is restless, and my alternate grumbles incessantly, and the house is too warm, and my mind is unsettled here, it edges towards the reckless and the river, towards moving home along the dark water, towards leaving all of this for a different time. I want to be gone.

They arrive, three of them, loudly, and it is just as well, for it gives me a chance to be angry, and my anger fixes me, points me front-wise, along the line I'm on, and before long they are chastised and we are organised, one bag on my shoulder, one on that of my alternate and the three heavies around the gentleman like an arrowhead. It occurs to me that this will raise a few eyebrows, and that perhaps just the two of us, early in the morning, might have gone unnoticed—but it is too late now for that. We move down the steps of the house and into the street, and we set a decent pace east, parallel to the river, with my alternate wondering out loud why we do not take a coach, and the heavies casting glances at children, and our gentleman a touch embarrassed, but as excited as a boy, his legs skipping a little on the stones, his sword hung beneath his coat, the bulge of it front and back both comic and grotesque.

I do not know what we look like. I do not know who sees us. Six men in procession through the back streets, making our way to the thin parts of the city, taking the leaking lanes and the cobbled, straw-strewn pathways, seeping out of the civilised world with all the waste and the wretched surplus, spilling out into the shallows, into the mud and the stagnant pools and the half swamps, into the sinking part of the island, the nearest to water, where we stand then, as if we have arrived at a centre, and we breathe deep and stand in a circle, and our feet are sudden wet, and our noses tight, and the gentleman amongst us claps his hands in fear and wonder, and exclaims, and I know not where he finds the words —

"By God it's worse than they told me, by God it is, what a wonderful worse it is."

And indeed it is. It seems to me that in a thousand years of trying you could not build a solid thing here, nothing lasting or secure. This is madness. The river here is invisible, in that it is everywhere, we are standing in it, it is level, it washes my boots with its black mud. My alternate gapes at me. One of the heavies laughs. But our gentleman notices nothing. He is gesturing at me for the bag, and I hand it to him, and he looks for a place to set it down, and has to balance it in the end on a bramble bush bare of leaves, and he rummages and mutters, and mutters and squints, and comes up with a measuring stick of polished wood, and I know that he wants to find a solid surface under us, a layer or rock or some such, and I know by the smell of the place that he'll need a longer stick than that. But he fiddles with it then, and I think for a moment that he is trying to snap it, but I see then that the stick extends—that it has been folded in on itself, and now he unfolds it, and it becomes longer and longer until it is maybe five yards, and thin but solid.

Beresford's men stand together, and I think they probably have a flask to share amongst themselves. My alternate has found a small rock, and has sat himself down upon it, gingerly, holding the tails of his coat out of the dirt, and he pulls up his knees and crosses his arms on them, and lays his head upon his arms, and pays no more attention to anything. I retrieve the second bag from his side, and I go next to the gentleman, and when he looks at me I help him with the measuring stick, which we push down together, using a clever cross wood-slotted to its end. He tells me to keep it straight, to watch his hands, to keep my own level with them. He stops a few times, and stands back and squints at the notches in the handle piece and at notches in the stick, and when he is satisfied that they are aligned, he allows us to continue. When we come to a halt, he makes a note in his pocket book. Then he pulls the stick from the ground, making his hands and his coat muddy. He walks some distance, and we repeat the procedure. We do this four times, over a wide area, and he would do it more, but is concerned at what little light we have left and remarks that the whole site will need proper measuring in any case. The pushing is very hard. It makes us grunt and sweat. The heavies simply stare at us, silently, their flask out in the open now, one of them with a pipe lit.

Of all the instruments he uses, and of all the tasks he performs, the measuring stick is the only thing I understand.

He retrieves various devices from the bags, and either puts them to his eye, or lays them on the ground, and makes copious notes. He has me walk through the mud some five hundred yards away from the river, holding another polished stick in my hand, and he peers at me through some complicated instrument which reminds me of those sextants a ship's navigator might use to fix himself against the stars, or the sun, or whatever they do. He waves at me and shouts, and has me move this way and that, and I can see that this is to the great amusement of Mr Beresford's men. My alternate appears to be dozing.

At this distance from him, from my gentleman I mean, I can see him against the city, with the sun going down in the west, and the shadows creeping out across the pools and the weeds and the scattered rocks. He is small. His group is small. I can see the far bank only as low land and the occasional building, and in the distance I can see the hills with their bright peaks, and to my left I can see the widening of the water and the falling away of the land. It has been this way for centuries.

I am baffled by what I do. I cannot grasp it. Something in my chest hangs heavy, like a dead branch, and I cannot lift it. I am unable to explain myself. This place is empty, it has always been so, but I have seen the gentleman's drawings, I have seen his plans, and I know what he intends to do here, and I no longer know where I am, I no longer know what this place is, whether it is barren and useless or whether it is more real in his mind than it is now in the last of the day, with the sun ending at last, leaving at last, giving up its watch. Where does this place belong? When does it belong?

When the light is too little we gather up his things and wake my alternate and set off again across the marshy ground towards the first paths. The gentleman is happy, his face is glowing, his eyes are bright. He sees what we do not, he occupies the future like a child, his plans are everything. So he does not appear to notice that a small crowd follows us from the edge of the lotts, and that the heavies, a little rough now with the liquor, are shouldering him along briskly, while my alternate and I swing the bags and bring up the rear. There is a man in the crowd whom I know, I do not recall his name, but he is a well-known city man and popular, and I can hear him at the back, his voice loud, crying "Shame," the same word, over and over, as if it is sensible, as if there is no need to explain it, as if everyone who hears will understand what he means. His rabble of men and boys call it too, and throw stones and laugh, and we move quickly through the streets, pushing guilt ahead of us, pursued by an anger that has its root in the future, clinging to a sorrow that is always present now.

My wife has prepared a meal for me, and the child is still awake, and I do not talk about my day—I eat and say nothing and I watch them at play. I wish to live with them. I wish to stay here in my home, with my family, to be present when my life comes to its end, to be here amongst the things I know and almost understand. I will not work for Mr Beresford any longer. Tomorrow I will go to him and say that he must find another keeper for his plans.

I am tired but I am afraid of sleeping. I repeat to myself that I am to quit my position, in the hope that it will influence my dreams and that I will not once more spend my night eavesdropping on the future, or on other times that are neither the future nor the past, but cracked views of the time I occupy. I am tired of the chronologies that compete and intertwine and which clutter my mind like weeds.

My son plays with pebbles on a board. He moves them and lets them roll, and determines where they rest by tilt and balance of the wood, moving his hands as if struggling with a great weight. I can see him deciding in his mind which way they will go, and I can see what he likes and does not like, and I can see that he likes to come close to dropping them, to let them run along the edge until it is almost too late, and then to save them with the smallest movement of his tiny hand. He is skilful at it. My wife sees me watching, and she smiles at me proudly, and I return her smile, and I think that we are happy here, by the river, the three of us.

I remember the woman who called, I remember the picture of her that I am left with, of her acceptance, her pride. It comes to me suddenly, unexpectedly, and I do not welcome it. There is too much evidence here, my head swims through it, and I wonder who she is, and I think of saying her name to my wife, but I do not want to tie one to the other, I do not want to mix the stories that flow here. I finish my food and I kiss my wife and my son and I go out of our home and I stand in the dark and watch the river.

I know that I am not being sensible, that I do not see things clearly, that my mind worries at loose threads, that I cannot find room enough for all that I see, all that I hear, all that I dream. I sit by the trough and look at the river, and I let my mind run on in the hope that it will tire itself, but it collects things, gathers them together, and the great mass that results is too big for me to contain, and I feel that I will burst, and that all the parts of me will be thrown to the river and there they will scatter and swim and that they will not—no matter how I desire it, no matter how I weigh them down—they will not drown. This is what I feel. That I will always swim the river. That I will always be there, separated out, made into essentials, never knowing my time, always in the river, my skinless mind, swimming the river, trying to find a standard time, a set place, a dry bank, a stopped city, a place to emerge, a complete place, to emerge again.

My wife comes out to me. She holds my shoulders and kisses my hair. We stand together silent in the dark, and we can hear, without wanting to, without listening for it, we can hear the city breathe, and sigh, and breathe, and continue.

Ross and Kinnder

THE HOUSE WAS IN DARKNESS but for one sullen candle in an upstairs window that flickered for a moment and died. Nothing then. Just the hum of the night and a distant clatter of hooves, some cart dragging noise through the streets.

I read my hands, turning them over and squinting at the backs of them, unsure of a word here and there but getting the gist. There was light from the moon, bits and pieces of it flowing down the edges of things at the corner of my eye, stopping when I looked, and in the near distance a new house was filled with a glow—a gathering started in the middle evening. I thought I could hear music, but perhaps not. There were coaches parked in the roadway, and a cluster of sedans, and men tended their horses while some heavies smoked at the gates and two old Charleys paced up and down swinging lanterns and coughing.

I counted to forty-eight, on the way to one hundred, and my mind drifted then and I lost where I was and started again and counted to thirty, and waited for a while and checked the street up and down and made my way across it, slipping into the shadows of the house, leaving the gate half closed as it had been, not touching it with any part of me. I counted the plants on the left, having to stoop to see if something was a plant at all or just a tuft of grass or rubble of clay, until I counted to the seventh, a big bushy thing up to my thigh, and I wondered what it was called and why it was called it, with its soft pale flowers and its scent like elsewhere oranges. I wondered because I wondered on top of it whether the name, or the story of the name, might tell me something about his reasons. For counting out shrubbery in the gloom is not an accurate thing, and it might have been managed better with a direction towards the first plant of the last plant, or the highest or the lowest. But he had clearly written the seventh. Which might in itself be the thing. But he is not a numbers man, does not pay any due to that, and I don't either, not that way. I am good at them and like to use them—like to count and measure and tally them up—they are easy company and good for the mind, and while I know they hold qualities and cruelties for some, for me they follow simply one after the other, as do the qualities and cruelties of any life.

At the foot of the seventh plant, half buried in the cold earth was a small leather purse containing the key of the house before which I stood. It was a small key for such a big house. I climbed the steps, six of them, gently, and found the lock and turned the key. There was nothing else to stop me. I clenched my heart and held my breath and stepped into the hall.

Cold. Dark and cold like a touch in winter and I couldn't understand that. Silent too, quiet as sleep, the hum of the night cut off like putting a lid on a jar. Not a sound. Lifeless. I waited, counting again, backwards, from twenty, slowly, moving my lips.

My eyes became useful, but not very useful. I picked out what I needed though—the stairway, and the door to the downstairs where the two housemaids would be sleeping and the old man would be turning and sighing through his wild dreams of horses. I saw the door to the Scottish woman's quarters, the lodger, solid shut. Timid, he had written, newly arrived and ill at ease. Nothing would bring her out. I put the key back in the purse and slipped it into the long pocket of my waistcoat. I peered at the walls and followed them, making my way to the stairs, sliding my feet onto the floor rather than stepping as such. Quieter. I pinched the cuff of my coat in my hand and touched it to the banister and carefully stepped up, afraid that my bones would crack, but they did not.

Slowly I climbed, concerned with my breathing and the gaps between steps, my head tilted always upwards, picking out the features of the landing. A portrait of her mother, a table with flowers, a waxy candle in a plain china holder, a vase on a three-legged table, doors. I paused near the top and tried in the gloom to read my hands once more, but there was not enough light coming through the battered slats of the stairwell window's splintered shutter. There was little money left here. No light, no money. I peered at the delicate black veins on my hands, at the latticework of what he wanted. I knew exactly what was written there, but I felt the need to see it again. Details compel me.

I slipped my security blade from its place in my sleeve and into my palm, snug. I call it my security blade because it's the one I would not be without, ever, under any circumstances. It's six inches, a snub point broken on bone, gleaming edges that rise and meet in the middle. Inch across, tapered. The handle is old wood, I don't know what kind, and it has my sweat soaked into it now so that it smells slightly. I had my initials on it but I scratched them out a year ago or so. I scratched some numbers then, but stopped.

I reached the landing and stood in the cold and waited and counted to fifty. Not a sound. Nothing from outside even. He said that she was a light sleeper and kept things quiet. Told me that the opening of her door would wake her because there was a creak in it and that there was nothing I could do about it other than hurry.

I reached fifty. Quick as I could I made my way across the landing, short steps. I opened the door with my free hand and did not pause. I glided across the room and reached the bedside as a flame rose in the lamp and the birth of a scream broke dribbling from her mouth and her face stared up at me like the face of a child. I got her hair in my fist and with my security blade I sliced her throat, at the same time trying to turn her away from me so that I wouldn't get the full force of the spray. It shot out all over the bed, hitting the floor beyond, and I could hear it. Her eyes rolled and there was a noise in her throat and she clutched at it but went limp very quickly. I stuck her in the back anyway, let her arch. There was quiet then and I felt her slump and I let her fall back down to form a pool on the bed and I moved away from her and checked myself for spray but apart from my hands and my cuffs, and a little on the corner of my coat, I was fine. I doused the lamp.

I spent a moment there in the room with her.

I used a sheet to clean myself and clean the blade, and I slipped it back into its place and quietly left the room. I counted my way across the landing and down the stairs and out the door. Twenty-three. They would not have heard a thing, the lodger in her fretful sleep, the maids clutched in the short dark, and the old man galloping, down in the basement. He rambles and is too old. But she keeps him on all the same. Or she did. He'll have to fend for himself now.

I drank gin in The Lost Child, enough to get me calmed down, relaxed, and made my way then over the river to The Broken Pony, near the cathedral. There was a crowd there and I was soon amongst them, listening to Rogue Murray tell an unending story of a ship's company wrecked and berserk on the coast of Spain. I had heard it before and it was no good. Long Pole was there, and his brother with the bad eyes, sitting in the corner whispering. They called me over but I didn't go. I saw John Lord Sweet and he bought me a drink and licked my ear like a puppy and wanted me to go with him out the back but I was fine after the woman and said no.

"Will you not Kinnder, no?"

"No John, I'm not right for it tonight."

"Ah Kinnder do me a favour and I'll be all nice."

"No John, I won't, so leave it now."

He sulked then and went off to sit with Long Pole and his brother and he tried his luck with the boy but the boy is nearly blind and assumes everyone is as ugly as Long Pole and keeps his mouth shut and looks after himself.

Maud came to me and told me that I had blood and writing on my hands and winked and slapped my arse. She's fat and smells of burning, but her face is friendly and I've never heard her say a bad word about anyone. She sells apples from a cart and stolen watches and small knives from inside her coat, down around The Blind Quay and the Custom House. She has a room somewhere filthy where she keeps cats.

"Will you be seeing Ross tonight?" Maud asked me.

"I don't know. Maybe. Why?"

Maud just shook her head and shrugged and moved off towards the fire where her sister stood swaying. Why had she asked me that? I knew I would not be seeing him. He would not risk it.

Outside in the gloom I found the pump and scrubbed at my hands, holding them up to the moon then to see what progress I'd made. I scrubbed them again and dried them in my handkerchief and held that up to the moon and saw a pink glow and a few dark smudges of ink.

"Will you touch me?" said a voice from the shadows, and I peered but couldn't make out who was there, and he or she didn't speak again and I went back inside.

Maud smiled at me as I came through the door and nodded and I didn't like it. It made me nervous. She drank with her sister and John Lord Sweet was with them as well, and Biggs and Royo and Mary. Long Pole and his brother were still in their corner, talking now to a gent who hovered uneasily beside them and then turned suddenly and laid eyes on Billy Coyle and grabbed him by the elbow and dragged him out to the street, Billy laughing, Long Pole shaking his head and making faces at his brother.

I stayed until the landlord took the stick out, and then left with Royo and stumbled down to Copper Alley where we chased a dog. Then he turned up towards the Castle and I turned towards the river and made my way home, spitting in the water and laughing to myself and throwing stones at any carriages that passed me. I got home and fell into my bed and stared at my hands and saw a smudge of things with only one world left that I could properly read. *Fleece*.

My head in the morning was like a wound.

I couldn't eat and my stomach fell out of me and I took until late afternoon before I was fit for a thing. I washed myself then and walked out as the sun was getting low, passing children playing on Queen Street and a dead horse by the markets. I followed the riverbank to the last bridge and stood for a while looking down at the Custom House, and the line of ships tied to the quay two deep all the way along, with four big ships tied together there by the bridge like they were one huge ship, and men and boys shifting cargo from the last one onto the others toward the quay. They flung crates and barrels like they weighed nothing, while sailors clung to ropes and hung above the decks like madmen, sorting through the sails as if they were looking for something lost.

I strolled like a gentleman along Parliament Street to the Royal Exchange, and on then up towards St Stephen's Green, taking long ways around and stopping at shops and tipping my hat. On King Street I met Crowley and he stopped me and asked me had I heard that Mrs Millington was dead, murdered in her bed, her throat cut and her heart ripped out.

"Her heart ripped out?"

"Aye, and blood on the ceiling Kinnder, imagine that though, blood on the ceiling."

"Her heart ripped out?"

"Oh yes, and half eaten."

"And do they know who did it?"

"I don't know Kinnder. They say though that she was the mistress of some gent."

"Who?"

"I don't know Kinnder. They say that this gent's wife

might have hired a fellow. Hired a butcher I'd say, by the state of her."

"Why?"

"Ripped apart she was, in several pieces in several places, like a chop shop the scene was, they say, it's what they say Kinnder, what I've been told anyway. And teeth marks Kinnder. Teeth marks."

His face was pale and he spoke in a quiet sort of voice, as if afraid that there might be some re-doing in the retelling. But there is not. What's done is done, and what was never done is words only. I did not want to smile, but I was seeing what I always see—that whatever horror takes place in the world, it is never enough. It will be puffed up until it shocks, and so the audience writes the plot, demanding teeth marks.

"I don't see that there's anything funny in it Kinnder."

"There isn't."

"It'd be a way of getting at them," he muttered.

"At who? What for?"

"Nothing Kinnder. Never mind. I'm assessing only and it makes you smile. I will leave you to your pleasantries."

And off he trotted, his hips swishing sideways and his lips pursed up and his coat swinging hard behind him. I laughed. But I wondered.

They were lighting the lamps. All along the Green, carriages were lined up, horses stamping and steaming and drivers busy with shovels and brushes. I saw one I knew but avoided him well and made my way to the corner and stood beneath the new tree and paced and tried not to look up at the house. I saw the lights lit in the windows nonetheless, and a maid come up from the basement and run off with a basket, returning later with it full of flowers. Where she got them I did not know.

It took an hour for him to appear, swinging his cane and dressed no different than he would usually be. He had a smile on him.

"Evening Kinnder," he said.

"Evening Mr Ross, Sir."

"Job well done Kinnder. Well done indeed. The talk of the town."

"Thank you Sir."

"Hold out your hands."

I held them out and he stuck his cane under his arm and took my hands in his and pored over them like a seer reading my lines, turning them over and staring at them and touching them gently, feeling for something.

"Good man," he said and let go, and turned and began to stroll.

"It's a beautiful evening Kinnder."

"Yes Sir, it is."

"The quality of the colour. See that sky Kinnder? that's the skin of God, stretched over us. It is the skin of God."

"Yes Sir."

"Did you use her?"

"I did Sir, yes."

"How?"

I glanced at him. He smiled but did not look at me.

"How, Kinnder?"

"In the usual way Sir."

He nodded and looked at the ground and continued strolling.

"Are you evil do you think Kinnder?"

"I wouldn't know Sir."

He laughed and slapped my back.

"Well said, Kinnder. Well said indeed."

"I know I'm not good Sir," I said.

"No, indeed. Not good. You are not at all good. But then …"

He stopped and looked around. Behind us there was no one but an elderly couple some yards distant, strolling like us, deep in conversation.

"Who could be good beneath the skin of God?"

"Yes Sir."

He took up strolling again.

"What age are you Kinnder?"

I didn't know, not really. I had to guess, and then I added to my guess.

"Twenty Sir, or so."

He was quiet for some time and we walked on together slowly until we came to the corner. Ross stopped and looked up and then turned and we started back the way we had come. He held his cane behind his back now and his steps were lazy enough to make him sway a little.

"We will die in this world Kinnder."

"Yes Sir."

"And awake in another. Beneath the skin of this life is the skin of another. Beneath the skin of God is the skin of Kinnder. And the skin of the world. And the skin of Mrs Millington. Do you see?"

"Yes Sir."

"Beneath the skin."

He paused and touched his hat as we passed the elderly couple. The man nodded but the woman seemed not to see.

"I will pay you what I said."

He handed me an envelope and I put it into my pocket and remembered the purse with the key and took it out and handed it to him. He looked at it, puzzled for a moment, and then found a place for it somewhere in his coat.

"Come now Kinnder," he said, and he led me to a bench in the shadow of a tree where there was little light. We sat down and he looked around and then for several minutes he looked at me, carefully, unblinking, like he was counting.

"Give me your hands."

He took them in his own and from his coat he took a pen of some kind, and in the darkness, where I could see nothing, he wrote in his small neat lines all the words that he could not say.

Leo Redmond could not understand it.

"It is beyond reason," he said. "The poor woman. God have mercy on her."

"Indeed Sir," I said, and nodded.

I stood in his office watching him eat soup. I was never sure whether he watched me or not, as his eyes were independent of each other and seemed to circle in his head and rotate in their sockets and be everywhere at once like walnuts in a cup.

"Did you know the lady Sir?"

"Lightly. I had met her at functions and so on, in Gardiner's house most recently I think—he supported her, I believe he gave her the house, bought it for her, some such arrangement. She was a friend of his sister's, lost her husband to a riding accident some years ago, was a quiet, gentle woman, contained, sensible. Why this should have happened I do not know."

"Might it be political Sir?"

Redmond looked up at me, or I believe he did. He raised his head and his eyes swirled and settled somewhere within range of my own.

"What makes you say that Kinnder?"

I shrugged.

"I cannot think of how. I don't believe so. I would not know where to fit it in, how to weight it up, give it motive, so on, but certainly, she was not unconnected. Architecture I would say Kinnder, more than politics."

He resumed his soup.

"I do not follow you Sir."

"I do not lead you Kinnder."

He sucked at his spoon, and I fancied that his eyes made the noise of bearings, a grind and rattle, that his eyes needed oiling and his belly needed filling, and that in time he would come to me for these things and I would gently give them, and that then he would be all right.

"Will I go Sir?"

"Do not sulk Kinnder, you are foolish with it, it does not suit you."

He scraped his bowl, and finished it, and took a sip or more of his claret, and leaned back in his chair. Over his shoulder I could see the river, and Essex Bridge, busy still, and beside the bridge the Custom House with the sun glancing off it from the west, and the ships that sat there, a clump of rope and sail and timber, and the lighters that came and went, and the small boats that passed beneath the bridge with their sails put down.

"It is what you are looking at Kinnder. Follow that. Perhaps it is nothing. Indeed, I would be appalled if there were to be any connection, but it is what happens if you try to move the heart of a man halfway down his arm, or indeed, the heart of a woman, or perfectly put, so on, the heart of a city, this city or any other, it bleeds to death, and us with it. Her heart was relocated they tell me."

"I had heard something of that Sir, though I do not believe it. The telling exaggerates."

"I had it from a medical man who visited the scene, so you may well believe it Kinnder. So it echoes the plans of some to relocate that."

He jerked his thumb over his shoulder, and I did not know what he meant. The river or the boats or the bridge or the Custom House or the winches or cranes or the cargoes or the bustle or the cries or the money in the air.

"And that, as you can plainly see, is a heart."

He stood and went to a cupboard to find his pipe, and I stared through the window and was angry that I did not fully understand what he was saying, and I knew that he would not be plain unless I came at it another way, so I dropped back and I waited, and as he resumed his seat and fell, finicky, his eyes clicking in their little tumblers, to the task of lighting the tobacco, I came at him again.

"May I ask you a question Sir?"

"What is it Kinnder?"

"Mr Ross Sir. Do you know him?"

Leo Redmond closed an eye and scratched his cheek.

"Which Ross, Kinnder? Billy Ross?"

"No Sir, I believe he's called Thomas Ross. Of Stephen's Green."

Redmond coughed.

"Thom Ross. Yes. I do. Why?"

"No reason Sir. A friend has started working for him."

He nodded, his pipe flaring, and seemed to stare at me. I waited for the thing to take light to his satisfaction, expecting to hear more, but when his hands were down he simply smoked, and contemplated me, or the view to each side of me, or above and below, his eyes being coins in a walking pocket.

"Would he be a good employer Sir?"

He said nothing for a long moment, and I had to resist the temptation to follow the direction of his apparent gaze, as so doing may have brought on in me a fit. I wanted to laugh. How can a man with loose eyes expect to stare out another? Eventually he stirred himself.

"What are you up to Kinnder?"

"Nothing Sir."

"Thom Ross has connections. He might be said to be on the side of the relocators, the heart surgeons, the butchers. I believe he has a friend in Beresford and hopes to win himself a seat in the Commons. So I do not like him. But aside from the business of the Custom House, if all else were equal and not in issue, I would say still that he is not a man to mix with. It is my opinion. No more than that."

He sat up.

"Now Kinnder. I have a gross of cases due on Tuesday from Liverpool and I will need to have some men to move half to the Castle and half to Kildare Street. And I do not want that fool you fetched me last time, I cannot spare that level of breakage. To ship a thing across a continent and then have it smashed on the doorstep is not to be tolerated."

"No Sir. I will see to it."

"And you will see to it also that you mark all the cases as they are unloaded and that you keep a careful inventory from there to the end, and that not a single one is relocated, you hear?"

"Yes Sir."

"Relocation is all in all a bad thing Kinnder. I will have the documents for you tomorrow. Call to me at the end of the day."

He closed his eyes, and I wondered if the dance changed

behind the lids, whether it slowed or quickened or ceased altogether.

"I'll tell you a story Kinnder," he said, in a quiet voice. "About Thom Ross. A strange little story I heard from a man who's sober and sane and no liar. And even still it is hard to give it credence. Heard from anyone else I would not suffer it a moment. But my source is intriguing, and his telling of it compelling, and I am forced to think that it may be true, or close to true."

He puffed his pipe but kept his eyes closed. Behind him, the sun's light had left the Custom House, and the shadows were coming up out of the water and the ground.

"It all happened when Ross was at the University, fifteen years ago or so, while Francis Andrews was Provost. Easy times then, more or less. I knew Andrews a little. For a scholar he was a no bad drinker. In any case, young Ross was by all accounts a clever fellow, though quiet and not very popular. He drank little, and did not gamble, but it was said of him, and widely, that he was a regular with the whores, and that his vices were not of the standard student variety, that they were a little more mature, by which I mean corrupted, a little more adult, a little more alarming. He was generous with his father's money, and seemed to enjoy the most those taverns, you know them I'm sure Kinnder, where all of life is bought and sold for the cost of a half-decent meal and some liquor. I remember that it was said that he would go to these places alone and seek out the worst kind of company, and that on occasion this brought him trouble, and there was at least one instance in which he was robbed and wounded."

Redmond shook his head slowly.

"I knew his father, Arthur, land in Offaly I think, dead now. A sloppy man, easily confused, alert only to whatever inconvenience or offence he himself might be causing. You could not shake his hand without his apologising for his grip being too tight or too loose. A good heart and a bad head become tiresome. But his son was a worry to him, more than a worry, he was all that he could not understand: careless of others, devoid of pity, of sympathy, empathy, or any feeling for that matter. Arthur became angry, which was not anger as you or I would understand it, but a flustered, female thing, of wailing and hopelessness.

"Young Ross had rooms at the University, and a brutish manservant who would follow him where he was not needed, and be missing in those places where you might think a gentleman would like some muscle at his side. Rumours were rife. Ridiculous, sordid rumours which Arthur could not believe in, but the consistency and regularity of which alarmed him. He determined to discover what truth there was in them.

"At one point the young man took a trip down to the estate in Offaly, to do a spot of hunting I imagine. While gone, his father set off to visit his rooms. He had trouble gaining entry apparently, having to physically remove his son's servant from the doorway. Once inside he began his examination, slowly, with an open mind, with some hope I imagine, and some trepidation too. I did not hear it from him, so I do not know how he took it, and I do not know the details of this first search, but I know that he did not have far to look for a first indication. In the main room, the sitting room, upon the table, there were drawings of an obscene nature, detailed, skilled drawings, but of subjects not fit for any civilised sketchbook that I can imagine, and writings, in his son's hand, that were sordid, depraved, internal."

Redmond laughed suddenly, and it seemed his eyes were out again.

"I can see Kinnder that you are shocked at the innocence of it all. What else, you rightly ask, would one expect to find in the rooms of a student these days. Well we are men of the world, and for all his weaknesses, so was Arthur Ross, yet he was deeply troubled by these first discoveries. And in any case, I have not finished, this is not all."

He stood and turned his back to me and looked out of the window as the light failed. I stared at his shadow as he spoke quickly, quietly.

"In the bedroom, in the bed, tucked up as if sleeping, was the body of a child, a little girl of no more than seven or eight whose throat had been cut and her blood drained, or had bled out, I don't know, in any case there was no blood on the sheets or anywhere else. Poor Arthur was violently ill. He left, and contacted a friend, the man who told me the tale, and they returned and discovered another body, again that of a child, in a trunk. This time there was much evidence of blood having been spilled. The servant had fled. He was not seen again. They debated it for a while and decided that the scandal would be too great. The children appeared urchins, skinny and unclean. They buried the bodies themselves that night in ground owned by the second man, near the river, and they searched the rooms further, removing all drawings and writings that Thom had made, fearing that there would be something in them to give him away. They removed also a quantity of opium and a large collection of children's clothing."

He turned and seemed for a moment startled at how dark the room had become. He peered at me, as if making sure that I was still there. Then he fumbled in a drawer and lit a match, lighting two tallow candles that sat on the table.

"Thom Ross went to America almost immediately, and there he stayed until after his father died, though Arthur was ill for a long time. He waited until his father was dead and his mother had gone to live in London with her sister before he returned. He had a brother I think, I don't know where he is, and there was a younger daughter whom I assume is in London also. He came back to the house in Stephen's Green, dismissed nearly all the staff and then hired only a basic household with I think only one maid. And he has changed all the furniture and fittings, paid a great deal for new plasterwork and artefacts of all sorts—imported from Italy and the Americas through Mr Donovan. Donovan tells me he spent a small fortune."

He sat down and poured himself some claret from a crystal jug.

"Do you believe the story Sir?"

His head was down and he did not answer for a moment. The light of the sky was gone.

"I don't know if I believe it. I don't want to. But the man who told me is an honest man, and I watched his face as he spoke the words. He seemed like a man who had buried murdered children in the darkness."

"Why did he tell you Sir?"

"I don't know Kinnder. Perhaps such a thing needs telling. For sanity's sake. After all, why am I telling you? You may have a need to tell another Kinnder, after a while. Choose well, that's all I say. Choose well. And once only, I beg you."

"I'll tell no one Sir."

Redmond drank and looked at me.

"Then you have a stronger heart than I Kinnder."

I had seen her often. I would collect her at odd hours and she would slip into the house on Stephen's Green by the back way once Ross had confined the servants to their quarters. He would meet her in the kitchens and they would go upstairs and stay there, for hours sometimes, while I paced the cold rooms downstairs and peered out at the street and drank his liquor. She was pretty. Black-haired and pale, and everything about her delicate and light. Her skin would shine.

I think it was because of her that Ross found me. I do not think she wanted to be collected by his carriage man or have to see his maids. I believe she asked him to find someone they could trust. So he found me in The Lost

Child and paid me and talked to me and gave me his trust
and his money in return for the nod of my head and the
look in my eye.

When they came down she would go to the sitting
room and he'd have me make tea and bring it in. I would
get the sedan then and take it around the back and she
would emerge and ignore me and climb in, obscured by
the black veil and the shadow, pressed into the corner like
a hiding child. I would take her across the city as far as
Thomas Street where I would turn then down Twatling
Street to the Barrack Bridge and across through Smith-
field and by that way through the back streets to her house
in Great Britain Street where she would not wait for my
hand but jump from her seat and disappear quietly into
the house. Sometimes the old man would come out to me
for a word. It was horses he loved he told me. As mad as
women, some of them, but more beautiful, he said.

Ross never spoke of her.

Mr Ross has never murdered children. I know him. I have
read what he writes on me. I have seen the way his mouth
is and the way his voice falters sometimes. I have felt the
way he touches me. There are questions that he always
asks, and others that he never asks. It is the way he skirts
around my work that tells me. He could not do it. That is
why he pays me. That is why he writes on my hands, and
sends my hands to murder, and touches my hands then
when the thing is done. My hands.

I spent an hour in The Broken Pony after leaving Redmond. Royo was there and he was full of himself. He talked at me and I did not listen. Instead I thought of what Redmond had told me, and I thought him a fool to believe it, as foolish as Crowley and all the others for whom simple killing was not enough, for whom the story had to grow in the dark parts of their heads, casting shadows on the places there where they did not want to look.

Billy Coyle approached me and wanted to know if Ross would be out that night. I told him no, and he seemed disappointed. I asked Billy if Ross had ever hurt him, or threatened him, or been odd or rough.

"Mr Ross is a lamb. He drinks milk and talks in pictures and falls asleep."

I was home early and ate a meal with Mary that I found I needed.

After midnight I removed my gloves.

In Ship Street they had knocked down the tower and rubble was strewn across the dark road and I stumbled twice and hurt my knee and cursed. I made my way forward nervously, looking out for lights and moving shadows. There was not a soul.

Leo Redmond paid me double, I do not know why. I think perhaps he made himself nervous with telling me the story of Thomas Ross. As for Ross himself, this is the third time this month that he has sent me out. I am flush. I will stay away from him for a while though, once I have collected the money. Three times in one month is too much. There is such noise about Mrs Millington that anything similar, even if it is only a whore or a beggar, will be noticed. And it is the first time ever that he has sent me out so quickly after one job to do another. Perhaps he is madder now than before. For I have no doubt that he is mad. How else could this be undertaken?

There was good light. I read my hands and saw the small picture Ross had made on my left palm, of Golden Lane and Friar Street meeting, and the figure in the gateway by the trough. In the mouth of Ship Street I stood in the shadow and peered at the little traffic of drunks and late men. A coach rattled by one way, and a sedan the other, drawing apart a silence from the point where they crossed, like curtains opening on a stage, revealing Long Pole in the gloom, hugging himself, shuffling.

I walked ahead and allowed my boots to make noise so that Long Pole looked up and smiled as I took out my security blade and held it beneath my coat and smiled back at him.

"Kinnder dear, what brings you up this place?"

"I was lonely Long Pole."

He lost his smile a little and was about to tell me not to joke with him, I'm sure, when I pushed him sideways into the shadows of a yard where timber was stacked and covered against rain. I pressed him up against the wood, and pressed myself up against him.

"Easy Kinnder, be gentle now. We'll soon have you sorted."

His hands were somewhere beneath my coat, the same place as my security blade, and they met a little and Long Pole cried out and jerked away.

"God Kinnder, careful with that bloody thing. I'm cut."

I took out the blade and moved to him, a great embrace.

"You are," I said.

Ladies wore their hair huge above them and some had their sedans altered to take the height. Others crouched and others rode like turkeys with their necks pushed out and their hair cutting the air before them. I sat on the bench and waited for Ross, my hands crisp now with Long Pole's blood, unwashed as they were, both of the blood and of Ross's writing, by order of Ross's writing. I kept them beneath my coat.

A servant girl smiled at me and I nodded. I must know her. I think I saw John Beresford on my way across the city, a slope-nosed man in conversation with a lady outside Lord Northland's house on Dawson Street. He was richly dressed and loud voiced and gestured quickly and I liked the look of him. I may leave Redmond and move down river with the Custom House—he will need men like me. Leo Redmond can go hang.

It was getting on for ten o'clock, and too hot for me, especially with my hands covered, before I saw him saunter down his steps and cross to where I was, wigged and frock coated, his skin very pale, perhaps powdered. He nodded, and regarded me for a moment, and again I was nervous that we would be seen there together. But what was written on my hands had to be obeyed, or I would have no money.

"Kinnder, good fellow. All done?"

He sat beside me and glanced at the sky.

"Yes Sir."

"Did you know him?"

"Yes Sir."

"Was he a friend of yours?"

"I don't know Sir. No, I wouldn't call him a friend exactly."

"That's good Kinnder, I'm glad of that."

He ran a finger along his brow. He was sweating.

"Did you do as I asked?"

"Yes Sir."

"Let's go in then."

He stood and walked off towards the house and I had to trot to keep up. He led me up the front steps and I kept my head down. Inside, the temperature was cool and I breathed in the air and was glad of it for once. Ross peeled off his wig and his jacket and threw them on a table. He led me to the sitting room where I had brought tea for Mrs Millington. Simple chairs surrounded a fireplace, and two tables held papers and bottles and a pipe. The room smelled sweet to me, of sweat and opium.

"Sit down Kinnder."

I sat on a hard chair, and after a moment with his face turned up as if looking towards a blemish on the ceiling, Ross dropped to his knees in front of me.

"Your hands Kinnder."

I held them out and he stared at them for a while, be-fore gently stroking them, his head swaying from side to side. Then he took my right hand in his cupped palms and seemed to read his own writing, breathing sharply and gasping a little, as if astonished. Then he bent forward and breathed once deeply, and exhaled a warm breath on my skin. I could see only the back of his head then, but I felt his tongue begin to lick my fingers and my knuck-les and my palm, becoming stronger until he was kissing and feasting on my whole hand, sucking from it the blood of Long Pole and the words that he had written that had drawn the blood of Long Pole and put it there. I moaned and closed my eyes and leaned back upon the chair and rested my hand as gently as I could upon my thigh. But he stopped then and picked up my left hand and started upon it with the same care and the same wildness. I could not help my moaning, but it was as if he did not hear me or notice my state. He carried on in a rapture of his own, cut off from all calling, all attention to the world, until he took both hands at once and tried to cram them into his mouth, and could not, and half screamed then, a ragged scream like a child in pain, and fell lifeless onto the floor, as if every strength had left his body, even the strength for thought and the strength for sending blood about the veins, and the strength for breathing.

I stared at my hands. They were as clean as though I had scrubbed them. All trace of Long Pole and of the instruc-tions was gone. My skin glowed and throbbed and shone and I thought of Mrs Millington.

Ross did not move. I thought he might have fainted. But his voice came then, thin and shaking.

"You may go now Kinnder. Thank you."

I touched my hands and stood, unsteadily.

"I'm sorry Sir, but the money . . ."

Ross stood slowly, as if in pain. On his feet he wiped at his mouth and looked at me.

"Of course," he said, but he did not move. He put a finger to one eye and coughed. I felt sorry for him then. He looked pale and unhealthy, and ruined by himself, and bewildered.

"I'll get it Sir, if you'll tell me."

"My jacket Kinnder. In the pocket of my jacket. An envelope."

I went and found the money and thought of leaving directly by the back door, but changed my mind, returning instead to the sitting room where Ross sat on a chair, his head in his hand.

"Sir?"

"What is it Kinnder?"

"I heard a story."

"Yes?"

"About you Sir."

He shrugged and looked at me. His eyes were wet.

"What about me Kinnder?"

"I didn't believe it Sir."

"Why not?"

"You are not that kind."

"What kind am I?"

"I do not know that Sir, I'm sorry."

"And what kind am I not?"

I went further towards him and sat where I had sat before. My hands still hummed to me, and I stared at them.

"It was said you had killed children, pauper children, while you were a student, and kept the corpses in your room."

He looked at me and his eyes changed a little, widened and dried. He sniffed and rubbed his chin.

"It is not true."

"I did not think it was."

"It is one of many things said about me Kinnder. That I am a devil. That I eat living things. That I live in a cellar and copulate with wild dogs and demons from the dead world. That I murder children. I do not murder children Kinnder. It's you who does that."

He did not smile. The room was cold again. My hands hummed. I have said that. The cleanest hands in the city. Long Pole dead by them, split open in a timber yard. For the first time then I thought of his brother.

"Don't say that Sir."

"Why Kinnder, not saying it will not silence it. I have known you to be the murderer of men and women and children. I have seen the blood on your hands. I have touched your hands. They are your hands."

I was silent, and I did not like the silence.

"How did we start this Kinnder?"

"I do not know Sir."

"Neither do I Kinnder. I have forgotten. Have you forgotten?"

"Yes Sir."

"Was it you who thought of it, or was it I?"

"I believe you hired me Sir."

"I believe I did. But what made me do that?"

I could not think. He had talked me into a trance and I had been sent out, written upon, and I had continued.

"I have the money Kinnder, that is all. The hands are yours. I have never killed a soul. I would not do it. I am afraid of hell."

He stood and left the room.

By the river I saw the ships tied down, their masts slung only with rope and the afternoon sky. On the Custom House quay a crowd had gathered by the crushed shape of a boy, held dying by a cage of corn sacks. I went to look, and knelt by him as his sweat and blood ran on the cobbles and the screaming left him for a soft muttering that filled me with fear.

"You are dying now," I whispered to him, and stroked his hair.

He gripped my hands.

Keith Ridgway

"Breathtakingly unpredictable and unapologetically strange."
—*The Guardian*

"Original and dramatic." —Colm Tóibín

"His stories are artful indeed—with a rolling, gathering cadence that is mesmerising. The circumstances he examines are wonderfully odd. Unusually for such a stylish, descriptive writer, Ridgway is also a master of action."
—*The Economist*

Keith Ridgway was born in 1965 in Dublin. His novella *Horses* appeared in Faber First Fictions in 1997 and was followed in 1998 by his critically acclaimed first novel *The Long Falling*, which has been awarded both the prestigious Prix Femina Étranger and Prix du Premier Roman Étranger in France. Ridgway's stories have appeared in various anthologies in Ireland, Britain, and the United States. His collection *Standard Time*, from which the stories collected here have been pulled, won the Rooney Prize in 2001. His most recent novel, *Hawthorn & Child*, was published by New Directions in 2013.